A GIFT FOR

FROM

This coupon is good for...

This coupon is good for...

This coupon is good for...

This coupon is good for...

This coupon is good for...

This coupon is good for...

This coupon is good for...

This coupon is good for...

This coupon is good for...

Made in the USA
Las Vegas, NV
01 November 2023

80007013R00037